WHERE'S WAFFLES?

Created by Barry Elwonger
Published by Little Ledger Press
'Big lessons from little stories.'

www.LittleLedgerPress.com

Little Ledger Press

ISBN 979-8-9987478-5-4

First Edition

In a house filled with laughter, joy in every space,
A corgi named Waffles loves to dash and race.
She's the hide-and-seek queen,
the best you'll ever see.

So, we start our search, whispering,
"Where, oh where could waffles be?"

In the playroom, there are
costumes, blocks, and games,
Lots of princess outfits, and even
dragons with flames!

"Where's Waffles?"
we wonder,
sipping on our slushies.
But nope, not here
just a fox-like stuffie!

Her tennis ball wobbles, then rolls into a nook.
We dart toward the hamper and give it a look.
"Where's Waffles?" we whisper, our hearts in our chest.
But the hamper is empty, so let's check the pantry next!

In the pantry, we spot something low to the ground.
Golden and toasty, and perfectly round.
"Where's Waffles?" we whisper, convinced we'd
soon meet...

BUT NO, IT'S NOT WAFFLES. IT'S JUST A LOAF OF WHEAT!

The backyard whispers secrets,
under the open sky,
"Where's Waffles?"
we wonder, as the birds sing and fly.

A small tail wiggles in the grass.
Could it be our girl?
But no, it's just a nutty little squirrel.

Back inside, the living room is cozy and warm,
Could Waffles be hiding from a passing storm?

Next we check Dad's office.
It's a messy little space.
A trophy on his desk reads
"Best. First Place!"

We dig through all the clutter,
we check everywhere.
But Waffles is missing.
She's just not in here!

The parents' room is next, a place
of rest and dreams,
Could Waffles be here, hidden in
the sunbeams?

The hallway is quiet as we
wander our way.
Waffles is so good at hiding.
We just want her to play!

Then... snrrk!
A small snore, gentle and near.
We lean in closer.
Could Waffles be here?

In the closet, a world of clothes and shoes,
We check a cozy corner,
and there, we find great news.

"HERE'S WAFFLES!"
we cheer,
our hearts echo in delight,
In her peaceful slumber,
she's a beautiful sight.

More Adventures Await!

Explore more books from the world of Little Ledger Press:

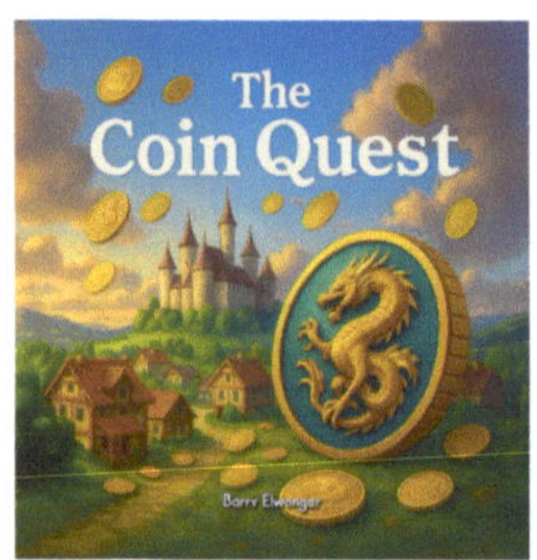
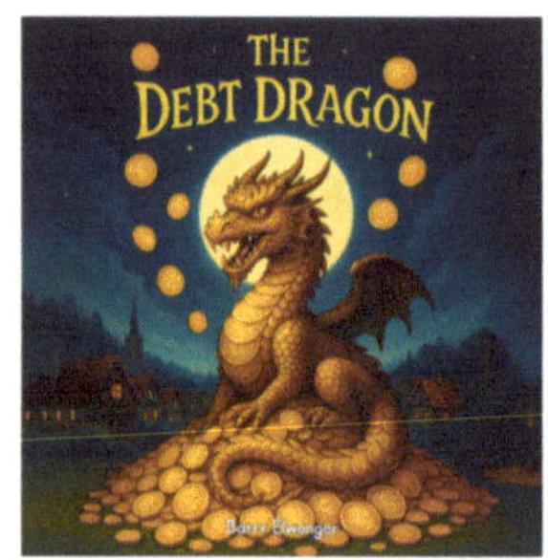

All proceeds from this book series go directly to support Brooke and Blake's college funds. Thanks for helping young readers dream big - and plan smart.

Little Ledger Press

For more books, resources, and free downloads visit:

www.LittleLedgerPress.com